THE
BEDTIME
STORY
BOOK

Illustrated by Angel Dominguez
Adapted by Jen Wainwright

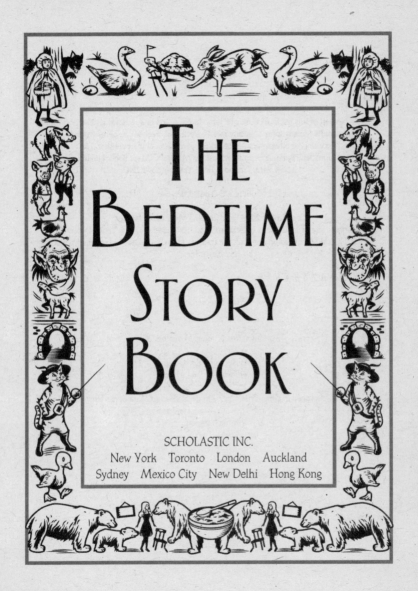

THE BEDTIME STORY BOOK

SCHOLASTIC INC.

New York   Toronto   London   Auckland
Sydney   Mexico City   New Delhi   Hong Kong

ISBN 978-0-545-32126-6

12 11 10 9 8 7 6 5 4 3 2 1   10 11 12 13 14 15/0

Printed in the U.S.A.   40

This edition first printing, November 2010

Cover design by Zoe Quayle
Cover image by Paul Moran

First published in Great Britain in 2009 by Michael O'Mara Books Limited,
9 Lion Yard, Tremadoc Road, London SW4 7NQ
www.mombooks.com

Contents

Introduction

Each of the stories in this book is perfect for reading aloud at bedtime. Traditional tales that are familiar favorites have been combined with lesser-known stories and fables from around the world that you and your children can discover together. This heartwarming collection of bedtime stories will be enjoyed by adults and children alike.

Goldilocks and the Three Bears

Once upon a time, there were three bears who lived in a little house in the middle of a forest. There was a father bear, a mother bear, and a baby bear, and they were very happy together.

One morning, the bears made a pot of porridge for their breakfast, but it was too hot to eat, so they decided to go for a walk in the forest while it cooled.

While they were out, a little girl named Goldilocks came upon the bears' house. She lived on the other side of the forest and had been sent on an errand by her mother.

However, Goldilocks was a naughty little girl, and she had spent her time chasing butterflies instead.

Goldilocks was also a very curious little girl, and she peeped in through the window. Seeing that the house was empty, she was bold enough to try the door. It was not locked, so she stepped inside.

She saw the bowls of porridge on a table, and her stomach began to rumble. Without stopping to think that this porridge did not belong to her, she sat right down and began to eat.

First, she tasted the porridge in the biggest bowl that belonged to Father Bear. "Urgh! This porridge is much too salty," said Goldilocks, and she wrinkled her nose.

Next, she tried the porridge in the medium-size bowl that was Mother Bear's. "Yuck! This porridge is much too sweet."

Then, she tasted the porridge in the littlest bowl, and her eyes lit up. "This porridge is just right," she said, and she ate it all up.

After she had finished gobbling up all of Baby Bear's porridge, Goldilocks spotted three chairs. She was tired after chasing butterflies, so she sat down on the biggest chair.

It was Father Bear's chair, and it was strong and wooden, but she could not get comfortable. "This chair is much too hard," she declared.

Then she sat in Mother Bear's chair, which was covered with plump cushions. "This chair is much too soft."

So, she sat in the smallest chair, which belonged to Baby Bear. "This chair is just right," she said, and sighed happily. But Baby Bear's chair was too small for her and it fell to pieces. Goldilocks landed on the floor with a bump.

She picked herself up and stamped her foot. She was still tired and now she had nowhere to sit down. Then she noticed the stairs leading up to the bears' bedroom, so up she climbed.

In the bedroom, she saw three beds: a great big bed, a medium-size bed, and a tiny little bed. First she lay down on the great big bed, but it was too high at the top. Then she lay down on the medium-size bed, but it was too high at the bottom. She found the littlest bed was just right, and she curled up in it and fell fast asleep.

Now, by this time, the bears had grown tired of walking and were ready to enjoy their breakfast. But as soon as they got back to their house, they could tell something was wrong, for Goldilocks had been careless and had left the spoons in the bowls of porridge.

"Somebody's been eating my porridge," growled Father Bear in his gruff, deep voice.

"Somebody's been eating my porridge," cried Mother Bear.

"Somebody's been eating my porridge," squeaked Baby Bear, "and they've eaten it all up!"

The bears knew that someone had been in their house, and they began to look for other signs. Suddenly, Father Bear noticed the cover of his big wooden chair was not straight. "Somebody's been sitting in my chair," he said.

Mother Bear saw that some of the cushions on her chair
had been squashed flat. "Somebody's been sitting in my
chair," she said. When Baby Bear saw his chair, he let out a
cry. "Somebody's been sitting in my chair, and they've
broken it to bits!"

The bears began to search their house. They marched
up the stairs to their bedroom. Mother and Father Bear
saw that the blankets on their beds were crumpled.

"Somebody's been sleeping in my bed," they cried.

Baby Bear was very shocked when he came to
his bed and saw Goldilocks curled up
fast asleep in it. Her yellow
hair was spread out
on his pillow.

"Somebody's been sleeping in my bed, and she's still in it!" he squeaked. Father Bear and Mother Bear both came immediately to see who it was who had broken into their house, and it was at this moment that Goldilocks woke up.

When she saw the three bears standing around the bed, looking down on her angrily, she was so frightened that she leaped out of bed and ran all the way home as fast as her legs would carry her. Goldilocks vowed that she would never let her curiosity get the better of her again.

The Ape and the Crab
(A story from Japan)

Once upon a time, in a far-off land, there lived a crab who made his home in the side of a sandhill. One day, an ape was passing by, carrying the seed of a persimmon tree. He spotted the crab, who was sitting in the sunshine enjoying a rice cake. Thinking that this looked like a tasty snack, the ape asked the crab if he would swap his rice cake for the seed he was carrying. Luckily, the crab agreed.

The crab set about busily planting the seed. He took great care of the little shoot that sprouted from it, and, soon enough, a glorious persimmon tree had grown up from the ground and was bursting with ripe fruit.

The ape came back to visit the crab one day. He was very impressed with the size of the tree and asked if the crab would spare him a few of the delicious fruits.

"I'll make a deal with you, my friend," said the crab. "I am only small, and I can't climb up the tree to reach the fruit.

If you will climb up and pick them for me, you may have half of the fruit from my tree."

The ape bounded quickly up the tall tree and began pulling the yellow and orange fruit from the branches. The trusting crab waited below, and his mouth watered at the thought of the tasty fruit that was coming to him. But the ape was cruel and crafty. Sitting high up in the tree, he stuffed the pockets in his fur with persimmons and then began selecting the ripest and juiciest. He crammed the flesh and pulp into his greedy mouth.

Each time the ape came across a green, sour persimmon, he would pull it off the tree and fling it at the crab on the ground below. The ape was so strong that the blows almost cracked the poor crab's shell.

The crab felt cheated and powerless as he watched the greedy ape. Suddenly, he had an idea. He waited until the creature had finished gorging himself and then called out, "You may think you're very clever, ape, but I bet that you cannot climb down the tree headfirst."

The ape had never once turned down a bet, and he did not intend to start now. "Ah, foolish crab," he said, "not only will you go hungry today, but you will also lose your bet."

With that, he began to descend the trunk headfirst. Of course, this was exactly what the crab had wanted to happen, because as soon as the ape turned himself upside down, all of the persimmons rolled out of his pockets and onto the ground, where the crab quickly ran around gathering them all up. When he had collected all that he could carry, he scuttled off back to his hole in the sandhill.

When the ape realized that he had been tricked, he was furious. He ran to the sandhill and lit a fire outside it, making sure that all the smoke blew down the hole into the crab's home. Eventually, the crab had to pull himself out, coughing and stuttering, before he was choked to death. But still the wicked ape was not satisfied. He kicked and punched the poor crab, and then scampered away, leaving the crab for dead.

The injured crab lay still, unable to move and too weak to call for help. After a while, he heard footsteps coming toward him. Three traveling companions — an egg, a wasp, and a rice mortar (a tool to grind rice) — were passing by the sandhill. They were very shocked to see the crab lying on the ground so obviously in distress.

Together, they picked him up and carried him inside the sandhill, where they soothed his wounds and put him to bed. Later, he told them the whole sorry tale. The three travelers were very angry when they heard how their new friend had been treated by the cruel ape, and they began plotting their revenge. While the crab rested, the egg, the wasp, and the rice mortar drank many cups of green tea and came up with a plan.

The next day, when they were all well rested, the three travelers took the bruised and battered crab and together they marched to the castle where the wicked ape lived.

The wasp flew up to the window and reported back to the others on the ground that their enemy was not at home — the castle was empty. This was perfect for their plan. They ran inside, and each found a place to hide and wait until the ape came back. The egg made itself a little nest among the ashes in the hearth and covered itself with soot until it was completely disguised. The wasp chose the bathroom for his hiding place. He flew inside a closet to await the ape's return. The rice mortar hid himself away behind the great wooden door of the castle, and the crab sat down by the fire and prepared to greet his enemy, the ape, when he came home.

When darkness fell, the ape arrived back at his castle. He lit a fire in the hearth to boil water for tea. "Dear crab," he said as he sat down by the fire, "you really are a foolish creature. Have you come to make another bet with me? Have you forgotten my victory over you already?"

At that moment, the egg hiding in the fire burst from the heat, spraying boiling yellow yolk all over the ape. It went in his eyes, leaving him scalded and nearly blind. He howled with pain and rushed to the bathroom to soothe himself with cold water. As soon as he got there, the wasp flew out of the closet and stung the ape several times on the end of his nose.

The ape was in a state of great pain and confusion—he felt surrounded by enemies. He began to run toward the door of the castle, while the wasp flew after him, stinging and taunting him. All of a sudden, the rice mortar revealed himself and chased the ape out of the castle, beating him soundly as he went.

The disgraced ape ran far away. There was no one in the land who would help him in his plight, as they all knew how crafty and mean he was. He was destined to wander alone for many years.

As for the crab and his companions, they celebrated their victory with much rejoicing. They had become such great friends that they decided to live together in the castle. The crab's wounds healed completely over time, and soon he was engaged to the beautiful daughter of a rich crab who lived in a neighboring land. They had heard the story of the crab's courageous battle with the wicked ape and were very impressed with his bravery.

On the crabs' wedding day, there was a great feast of delicious persimmons, and everyone ate and drank their fill. Soon after the marriage, a new baby crab was born. The little one loved to play with the rice mortar and the wasp, and they all lived together as one happy family.

The Emperor's New Clothes

(Adapted from the story by Hans Christian Andersen)

Long ago, there lived an emperor who was very vain. He wanted only the best and finest things, and had a great many rich clothes of silk and velvet. Indeed, he loved dressing in elegant clothes so much that he wore a different outfit every hour.

Two crooks had heard of the emperor's vanity and came to the palace with a cunning scheme to trick him. "Greetings, Your Majesty," they said. "We are two skilled tailors, and we would be honored to make a suit of clothes for you. It will be unlike anything you have ever worn, because our clothes are not only beautiful and fine, they also possess a magical quality. They can be seen only by men of intelligence and worth—to anyone stupid they will be invisible."

"How marvelous," the emperor thought to himself. "If I had these clothes, I would be able to tell who in my empire was clever and who was stupid." He told the two tailors to begin the suit at once and gave them many gold coins as payment.

The two scoundrels sent for expensive silks, and gold and silver

thread, which they quickly put into
their pockets and kept for themselves.
Then they set up their looms and made
a great show of starting work, even though
there was really nothing on their looms at
all but empty air.

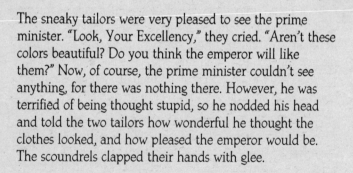

After a few days, the emperor called for his
prime minister, a wise and honest man, and
told him to go and see how the new clothes
were coming along.

The sneaky tailors were very pleased to see the prime
minister. "Look, Your Excellency," they cried. "Aren't these
colors beautiful? Do you think the emperor will like
them?" Now, of course, the prime minister couldn't see
anything, for there was nothing there. However, he was
terrified of being thought stupid, so he nodded his head
and told the two tailors how wonderful he thought the
clothes looked, and how pleased the emperor would be.
The scoundrels clapped their hands with glee.

Soon enough, it was time for the emperor to have his
measurements taken for the new suit of clothes. The tailors
approached the emperor, pretending to hold armfuls of the
cloth they had made. "Come closer, Your Highness. Feel
how soft this fabric is. See how intricate the stitching is.

We have worked for many days and nights on these clothes, so we hope you are pleased with them."

The emperor felt his heart begin to race. "Good heavens," he thought. "I can't see the cloth at all. This must mean that I am stupid!" Deciding right away that no one must ever know, he began to praise the tailors loudly for their skill. Immediately, the room was full of voices saying how beautiful and fine the clothes were, for not one of the emperor's advisers wanted to admit that he could not see anything there. The tailors looked at each other and smiled as they took the emperor's measurements. Then they began cutting the air with scissors and pretended to sew together the clothes. Their plan had worked.

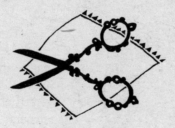

News of these wonderful clothes and their special qualities spread through the city, until everyone wanted to see them. The emperor decided to show off his new clothes in a great and regal procession, and a huge crowd gathered in the streets. All the people were eager to find out if they could see the clothes or not. They also wanted to see which of their neighbors would be revealed as stupid or ignorant.

Back at the palace, the emperor dressed himself in his new clothes and stood looking admiringly at himself in the mirror. He was a little worried about showing himself off to his subjects, since he still could not see the clothes. However, the crafty tailors assured him that he looked magnificent, and all his servants in the palace agreed with them. So, he decided to take their word for it.

The royal procession left the palace and began to move through the streets of the city. The emperor strode along proudly at the front, with his advisers at his side.

As they passed, applause

broke out among the crowd of people, who all began jostling to get a better look at the emperor and his new clothes. A murmur of voices rose from the crowd, loud enough for the emperor to hear as he walked along.

"Look at the emperor. Aren't those clothes amazing?"

"Oh, the colors, such wonderful colors!"

"And how well they fit him."

You see, no one in the whole city wanted to admit that they could not see the clothes. So the citizens all pretended that they could — each one in a louder voice than his neighbor.

All of this was music to the emperor's ears. He basked in the praise, feeling elegant and handsome, and thinking what intelligent subjects he had.

Suddenly, a child's voice piped up from the crowd.

"The emperor is naked!"

The boy whose voice it was did not care about being thought clever or stupid. He said things exactly as he saw them, and once more he cried, "Look! The emperor is naked."

Everyone in the crowd heard this, and the boy's remark was repeated over and over again. The people of the city looked again at the emperor, and soon everyone was shouting, "The boy is right. The emperor is naked!"

The emperor realized that his people were right—he was not wearing any clothes at all. But still he was too proud to admit to it. So, he carried on with the procession through the streets, with the people's laughter ringing in his ears.

The Ugly Duckling

(Adapted from the story by Hans Christian Andersen)

It was summer, and everything was green and blossoming. In the heart of the countryside stood an old farmhouse, next to a deep river. On the banks of this river, a mother duck was sitting on a clutch of seven eggs.

She was getting rather tired of this. Her children were in no hurry to come out of their eggs and greet the world. But suddenly, one by one, the eggs began to crack open and out popped six fluffy, yellow ducklings that all began quacking as best they could. The mother duck could only remember laying six eggs, but there beside her was a seventh egg. It was bigger than the others, and had still not hatched. Soon enough, the seventh egg popped open, and a strange-looking duckling with gray and brown feathers emerged.

"Goodness," thought the mother duck. "How can that ugly duckling be one of my children? He looks so different from his brothers and sisters." But the ugly duckling was a good swimmer, and was kind to the other ducklings, so she looked after him and treated him as one of her own.

The strange-looking duckling had a huge appetite. He ate far more than any of the other ducklings, and soon he had grown much bigger than they.

Sadly, all the other animals in the farmyard were very cruel
to the duckling. They laughed at him because he was
clumsy, and jeered at him because he was ugly. The geese
pecked him, the chickens clucked at him, and the girl
who fed the animals kicked at him when she passed.
The ugly duckling felt so miserable and unloved that
one day he ran away from the farm.

Everywhere he went, the duckling asked if anyone knew of
any other birds that looked like him. But he always got the
same response, "No, we don't know anyone as ugly as you."

Then one day, his travels took him to an old woman's
house. This old woman did not have very good eyesight, and
she caught the poor duckling, thinking he was a stray goose.
She put him in a hutch, hoping that he would lay lots of
eggs for her to eat. Of course, because he was a male
duckling, this was impossible. Every day, the old woman's
cat would taunt him. "If you don't lay some eggs soon, the
old woman will put you in a pot and roast you for her
supper."

One night, the old woman forgot to lock his hutch, and the duckling escaped. He fled as far away as he could. At dawn, he found himself in a thick bed of reeds, where he hid.

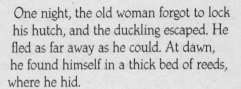

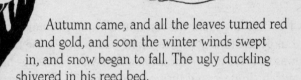

Autumn came, and all the leaves turned red and gold, and soon the winter winds swept in, and snow began to fall. The ugly duckling shivered in his reed bed.

One evening, as the sun was setting, a flock of majestic white birds with long, slender necks flew overhead. The duckling did not know what kind of birds they were, but he thought they were the most beautiful things he had ever seen. "Oh, if only I could look like them," he said wistfully. "Even just for a day, I would be the happiest bird alive."

As the winter got colder, the river and the reed beds began to freeze. The ugly duckling had to paddle harder and harder with his feet to keep himself from getting stuck in the ice. Each night, the space he had to swim in got smaller and smaller until finally, exhausted, he gave in and was caught in the frozen river.

A farmer walking by the banks of the river saw what had happened and felt sorry for the poor duckling. He broke the ice with his shoe and carried the cold bird home to his wife and children. The farmer's family treated him with kindness. Their house was warm, and he was given plenty of food.

The duckling spent the rest of the winter in comfort there, but by the time spring came, he had grown so big that it was time for him to move on once again. His wings had grown stronger, and they carried him high above the farmer's house and over the fields and hills until he came to the edge of a pond.

The duckling could not wait to get swimming again, and he raced toward the water's edge. Suddenly, he noticed that he was not alone. Gliding elegantly around the pond were three beautiful swans.

The poor duckling felt very unhappy. "All I wanted was to swim in this lovely pond," he thought. "Now these birds will surely peck at me and tease me because I am so ugly."

He swam out onto the water and lowered his head. He waited to hear the cruel words of the swans, but none came, and what he saw in the water amazed him. He stared and stared at his reflection. No longer were his feathers stubby and gray; no longer was he ugly. The bird staring back at him was a beautiful, white swan. He approached the other swans and, to his joy, they welcomed him as one of their own. Finally, the ugly duckling had found where he belonged, and he thought his heart would burst with happiness.

The Musicians of Bremen
(Adapted from the story by The Brothers Grimm)

There was once a donkey who had worked for a miller for many years, carrying sacks of corn and grain to the mill. But he was getting old and was no longer as strong as he used to be. The donkey could tell that his master was becoming displeased with him, and feared what would happen to him when he could no longer work. So, the donkey ran away and headed for the town of Bremen, where he thought he would try to join the town musicians.

Along the road, he came across a dog lying on the dusty path, panting. "My good fellow," said the donkey, "what on earth are you doing out here, so far from home?"

"I am old and weak, and I can't hunt the way I used to," whimpered the dog. "My master wanted to kill me because I am no use to him, so I ran away. Now I have no home and no place to go."

"Well, I am going to Bremen to be a town musician," said the donkey. "Why don't you come with me? I can play the guitar, and you can play the drum."

The old dog thought this was a fine idea, and the two of them trotted onward down the long road toward Bremen.

Soon, they saw a cat sitting on a wall and looking very forlorn. "What's the matter?" asked the dog, who was concerned to see another creature looking so miserable.

"I don't know what to do. I am not quick enough to catch mice anymore, and my mistress is very angry with me," said the cat sadly. The two hopeful musicians looked at each other when they heard this, and smiled. In no time at all they had convinced the old cat to join their little band, and the three of them were on the road once more.

Before long, they passed a farmyard. They stopped to admire the voice of a rooster who was sitting on the fence, crowing with all his might. "You have a fine voice indeed, my friend," said the donkey. "Why are you singing so loudly?"

"I heard the cook say that I am to be the family's dinner on Sunday, so I am crowing my heart out now, while I still can," said the rooster.

The three friends decided very quickly that a bird with such a strong voice would be a fine addition to their band. The rooster took very little persuading to run away with them, so off they went.

The town of Bremen was still a great distance away when the sun began to set. The travelers realized they would need to find a place to stay for the night. As darkness fell, they found themselves in the middle of a forest and felt very frightened. In the distance, the rooster noticed a glimmer of golden light through the trees. As they drew closer to it, they saw that it came from a house in a clearing.

As they looked inside the house, the little band saw a group of robbers sitting around a table that was laden with delicious food. The traveling animals were all very hungry, and each one groaned with delight when he saw the mouth-watering things that the robbers were eating and drinking. The donkey, the dog, the cat, and the rooster put their heads together, and soon they had come up with a plan to drive the robbers out of the house.

The donkey trotted up to the window, and the dog jumped up onto his back. Then the cat climbed up on top of the dog, and finally the rooster flew and perched on the top of the pile. Then, all at once, they began to sing. The rooster crowed, the cat meowed, the dog howled, and the donkey brayed.

The robbers were terrified by this sudden noise. They thought their house had been invaded by ghosts and they ran into the forest, screaming. The travelers were very pleased with themselves. They walked calmly into the house and sat down at the table. Then there was no noise for a very long time—apart from their contented chewing and swallowing, of course.

After their huge dinner, the four friends were very tired. Each of them curled up to get some sleep. The donkey lay down outside the house, the dog chose a spot behind the door, the cat curled up on the hearth, and the rooster flew up to perch on a beam in the roof. In no time, all four were fast asleep.

By this time, the robbers were feeling ashamed for being so easily scared. They decided to send one man back to the house to find out what had happened. The robber found the house in darkness when he got there.

He crept into the kitchen to light a candle. Thinking that the shining eyes of the cat on the hearth were glowing coals, he held out his candle to light it. The cat did not like this one bit, and he jumped at the man, spitting and scratching at his face. The robber screamed and ran for the door, but as he did, the dog awoke and bit him on the leg. Limping out into the yard, he was kicked by the donkey. As the robber ran shouting into the forest, the rooster flew after him, crowing at the top of his voice.

When the robber reached his friends, he was in a terrible state. "Run!" he yelled. "There is a terrible witch in the house, and she scratched me with her claws. Then an evil spirit bit my leg, and a monster hit me with a club."

The robbers ran for their lives and vowed never to return to the house again. The animals were very happy with this. They were safe and warm, and the robbers had left behind plenty of food and provisions. They decided not to travel to Bremen after all, and lived together happily in that house for many years.

The Boy Who Cried Wolf

(Adapted from the fable by Aesop)

Once there was a boy who lived in a village in the
countryside. He was always looking for things to entertain
him, and would quickly tire of any activity that was given
to him.

One day, his parents had had enough of him complaining
that he was bored. So, they sent him up onto the hillside
to watch over the flocks of sheep that grazed there. "If you
want to do something, then you can do something useful,"
said his mother. "Go and find a nice spot to sit, and look
after the sheep. The fresh air will do you good, and you
can call us if anything happens."

Reluctantly, the young boy went off up the hill and found
a spot of soft grass under a tree to sit on. It was a beautiful
day, but the boy soon got bored of watching the sheep and
decided to play a trick on his parents in the village below.

"Help!" he shouted, at the top of his voice. "Help! There's a wolf coming to eat the sheep, come quickly!"

Soon, he saw a stream of people running from their houses and up the hill to help drive the wolf away. When they reached him, puffing and panting, they realized that there was no wolf. The looks on their red faces made the naughty boy burst out laughing. "I'm sorry," he said. "I couldn't resist joking with you." The villagers didn't think his joke was very funny at all and went back down the hill, shaking their heads angrily.

Before too long, the boy was bored once again. "Help!" he shouted. "There's a wolf coming to eat your sheep!" Sure enough, the villagers stopped what they were doing and ran up the hill to the boy's aid. He laughed and laughed until his stomach hurt. "I'm sorry," he said, once he had managed to get his breath back. "It was just too tempting to trick you all again."

Without a word, the villagers turned and went back to their houses, leaving the boy alone again. Suddenly, the boy saw a big, black shape slinking between the trees, and his heart started to race. "Wolf!" he called, as loudly as he could. "Come back! There's a wolf coming to eat the sheep!" But no one came. All the doors to the houses stayed shut. You see, the villagers all thought he was trying to trick them again. So the wolf ate the entire flock of sheep. And the boy never cried "Wolf!" again.

Puss in Boots

(Adapted from the story by Charles Perrault)

Once upon a time, there was an old miller who had three sons and very little money. When the old man died, he left his sons everything that he had. He gave his mill to his eldest son, his faithful donkey to his middle son, but to his youngest son he left only a cat.

The youngest son was very disappointed with this. "What on earth am I supposed to do with just a cat?" he complained. "My brothers can put their gifts together and earn a living, but this cat will bring me nothing but bad luck and poverty." The cat, who was a very clever animal, heard this and hated to see his master so sad.

"Don't worry, sir," said the cat. "All you need to do is get me a bag and a pair of boots, and you will see that your luck is not so bad after all." The young man decided he had nothing to lose and did as the cat asked.

The cat strode off through the fields in his boots, with his bag over his shoulder, until he came to a rabbit warren. He filled his bag with sweet grass and parsley, then crouched down at the entrance to the burrow and waited. Soon enough, the smell of the fresh grass drew a plump young rabbit out of his burrow, and he hopped into the bag. Quick as a flash, clever Puss in Boots pulled the drawstrings tight and caught the rabbit.

Right away, Puss went to the palace and asked to see the king. Bowing low, he presented the king with the fat rabbit. "Your Majesty, I present to you this rabbit as a gift from my master, the Marquis of Carabas," he said. This was a noble title that the cunning cat had made up, for his master was really no more than a poor miller's son. The king was very grateful for the gift and asked the cat to send thanks to his master.

The next day, and every day for the next few weeks, the cat returned to the palace with rabbits, partridges, and other delicious gifts that he had caught in his bag. Each time he gave them to the king, telling him that they were from the Marquis of Carabas. The king was very thankful for all of these gifts and decided that the marquis must be a great and generous man.

One day, Puss in Boots heard that the king and his beautiful daughter were going to take a carriage ride along the river. He ran to his master, saying, "Sir, I have a plan. Do as I say and you will be very rich." He told the miller's son to go and bathe in the river. While the young man was washing, the crafty cat took his ragged clothes and hid them under a stone.

As the king's carriage passed by the river, Puss ran up to it, shouting, "Help! The Marquis of Carabas is drowning."

The king recognized Puss in Boots and ordered his men to go and help. As the men splashed into the river toward the miller's son, the enterprising cat told the king that while his master was washing, a band of robbers had stolen his clothes. He added that although he had run after them, he could not catch them before they disappeared.

The king was very sad to hear this news. He sent for an elegant suit from the palace for the marquis to wear. The young man looked so handsome in these fine clothes that the king's daughter fell in love with him as soon as she saw him. He was asked to join the king and his daughter on their carriage ride, while his faithful cat ran on ahead.

Marching off in front of the royal carriage, Puss in Boots came across some workers mowing a field. "The king is coming," he said. "When he asks you who your master is, you should say that it is the Marquis of Carabas. Do this, and you will be rewarded." Every time he passed a group of workers, he told them the same thing, and, sure enough, they did as they were told and said to the king that they worked for the Marquis of Carabas.

Now, the king was seriously impressed with the wealth of the marquis and the amount of land that he owned. Seeing the way that his daughter looked at the young man, he began to wonder if he might be worthy of her hand in marriage.

Up ahead, Puss in Boots had reached a magnificent castle, which belonged to a fearsome ogre. The cat took a deep breath, for he was rather nervous about the next stage of his plan, and knocked on the castle door. When the huge ogre answered, the cat bowed very low. "Greetings, good Sir Ogre. I was just passing this way and felt it would be rude not to pay my respects to you."

The ogre grunted rudely, but nodded that the cat should come inside. "Now, Sir Ogre," said Puss, "your special powers are well-known throughout the land. I have heard that you are able to turn yourself into any animal, be it lion or elephant."

"That is certainly correct, and I know of no other with powers as wondrous as mine," boasted the ogre.

"Well," said Puss, with a glint in his eye, "I have a challenge for you. I have no doubt that you are skilled in turning yourself into big and terrifying animals, but I bet that you can't transform into something much smaller than you are, such as a mouse, for instance."

"How dare you doubt me?" roared the ogre angrily. "Just you watch this!" Before Puss's eyes, the enormous ogre shrank down to the size of a mouse. In the blink of an eye, Puss pounced on him and gobbled him up, leaving the castle without an owner.

Puss in Boots opened the door of the castle wide, just in time to see the king's carriage pull up outside. "Welcome, Your Majesty, to the castle of the Marquis of Carabas," he said. "You and your lovely daughter are welcome here as long as you like."

The king was so pleased with what he had seen that he made up his mind to make the marquis his son-in-law. He invited the young man back to the palace and arranged for him to be married to his beautiful daughter the very same day. The miller's son was overjoyed. He was forever more known as the Marquis of Carabas, and he and his bride lived together very happily. He never had to worry about being poor again, all thanks to his clever Puss in Boots.

The Grasshopper and the Ant
(Adapted from the fable by Aesop)

One hot summer, there was a grasshopper who spent all his time singing. He would sit in the long grass and perform all of his favorite songs in the sunshine. He loved the long, lazy days and the compliments he received on his fine voice.

One day, he saw a line of ants trudging past him. Each one was carrying a heavy load of grain on his back. "My friends," he called out cheerfully, "why are you working so hard? Put down your heavy load and come and enjoy the sunshine."

The ants shook their heads and carried on walking in the scorching heat. "We can't afford to stop work. We have to gather this food now and store it for the winter so that we don't go hungry."

"You worry too much," said the grasshopper, warming up his voice to begin singing once again. "There is plenty of time before the summer ends to prepare for the winter. You should relax and have some fun while the weather is fine."

The ants looked at one another knowingly and shook their heads. "You can relax if you like, but we know what we need to get us through the winter."

The grasshopper kept singing each day, and he was so caught up in making his music that he didn't notice when the leaves turned red and gold, or when the winter winds began to blow.

Before too long, the poor grasshopper was shivering with cold, and starving. As the snow began to fall, he could find nothing at all to eat, though he searched as hard as he could in the frosty grass. His search took him to the door of the ants' house, which looked warm and cozy. When he looked through the window, he could see the ants sitting around a table and eating a huge dinner. Right away, the hungry grasshopper knocked on the door.

"I am cold and hungry," he said. "May I please come in and share your food?"

One ant looked closely at him. "I recognize you," he said. "Weren't you the one who told us there would be plenty of time to store up food?"

"I was wrong," said the grasshopper sadly. "I spent all my time singing, and now I have nothing to eat."

"Well, I see you learned your lesson," replied the ant. "If you want to share our food with us, then you'll have to sing for your supper."

The Golden Goose

(Adapted from the story by The Brothers Grimm)

There was once a man with three sons. The eldest son was clever, the middle son was handsome, but the youngest son, whose name was Ernest, was neither especially clever nor fine to look upon. His parents and his brothers teased him and sneered at him.

The family needed some wood for the fire, so the eldest son was sent off into the forest to chop some. His mother made him a sweet cake and gave him a bottle of delicious apple cider so that he would not get hungry or thirsty while he worked.

Off he went into the forest and found a suitable-looking tree to cut down. But before he could begin, an old man with a long gray beard came up to him.

"Good day, young man," said the old fellow. "I am so very hungry and thirsty; would you give me a piece of your cake and a small gulp of your cider?"

The clever son thought about this for a moment. Then he replied, "No, for if I gave this to you, then I would not have enough for myself. Go away and find your own food to eat."

The old man went away, sadly shaking his head, and the clever son began chopping down the tree. After only a few minutes, he swung his ax too wide and injured his arm. He had to go home right away so that his mother could bandage it up.

The middle son then went into the forest to chop wood for the fire. His mother gave him a rich cake and a bottle of fresh apple cider to take with him. As he was preparing to cut down a tree, he heard a voice behind him. It was the old man with the long gray beard. He asked the handsome young man for a morsel of his cake and a drink of his sweet cider.

The second son looked down his nose at the old man and sent him away empty-handed. He had not gotten very far with his chopping when he struck himself on the leg with his ax and had to hobble home to let his mother tend to his wound.

Now, Ernest decided that it was his turn to try fetching the wood, but his father was reluctant to let him go. "Both of your brothers have hurt themselves—what makes you think you will do any better?" But Ernest kept asking and, finally, his parents gave in. "Go on then," said his mother. "But don't blame me if you get hurt." She gave him a hard, dry cake and a bottle of old, sour cider to take with him.

When Ernest got to the forest, he met the old man, who asked, "Please, young man, I am so hungry; may I share some of your food and drink?"

Ernest replied right away, "I have only dry old cake and sour cider, but you are welcome to share them with me." The old man was very grateful, and when Ernest unwrapped his cake and opened his drink, he found it had magically transformed into rich cake and fine apple cider. Together, they ate and drank their fill. When they had finished, the old man said, "You are a good-hearted boy, and your kindness will be rewarded. If you go to that tree over there and chop it down, you will find a goose with golden feathers hiding in its trunk."

Ernest did as the old man said and, sure enough, there sat

the golden goose. He picked it up and carried it under his
arm to a nearby town, where there was an inn in which he
decided he would spend the night.

The owner of this inn had three daughters. When they saw
the goose, they were amazed at how beautiful it was, and
each of them wanted to take one of the golden feathers for
herself. The three sisters planned to steal feathers from the
goose while Ernest was asleep. So, late that night, they crept
into his room and approached the golden bird.

The eldest girl reached out to pluck a feather, but as soon as
her hand touched the goose, she stuck to it. No matter how
hard she tried, she could not get free. Her sisters ran to help,
but they, too, stuck tight as soon as they touched her.

When Ernest woke up the next morning, he was surprised to see the three girls stuck to his golden goose. Nevertheless, he took the goose and went on his way about the town. The innkeeper's daughters had no choice but to run after him, following wherever he went.

Very soon, the town clergyman spotted this odd-looking procession. He was shocked at the actions of the girls and thought that it was not polite or proper for young ladies to run around after a man. He grabbed the youngest girl's hand to pull her away, but he stuck to her and was dragged along behind Ernest, his goose, and the girls. The same thing happened to the butcher, the baker, the blacksmith, and the washerwoman, until there was a long chain of people winding through the streets of the town.

On the edges of the town was the royal palace, where the king and his daughter lived. The princess was very

beautiful, but she suffered from a strange illness. Ever since she was born, she had never smiled or laughed. Her mouth was always turned down at the corners. The king was very troubled by this problem, and he vowed that any man who could make his daughter laugh would be granted her hand in marriage. So far, no one had been successful.

On the day that Ernest was leading his wild-goose chase, the princess was riding through the town in her carriage. As soon as she saw the strange procession being dragged through the streets, her face broke into a smile. Then she burst out laughing. It was a beautiful sound, and the king was overjoyed.

The king asked Ernest to come with him to the palace, and Ernest and the princess were married. Ever since that day, the palace has been filled with laughter.

The Three Little Pigs

Once upon a time, there were three little pigs. After a long summer of playing games and having fun, they decided it was time to settle down and build their own houses. They left their home and their parents and went off into the world to seek their fortune.

The first little pig was lazy by nature. He decided to build his house as quickly as he could. He gathered together bales of straw and, in no time at all, he had built himself a little house. He was very pleased with himself, and he called his brothers over to admire his handiwork, but they were not very impressed.

"That house is no good," said one. "It's much too flimsy."

"Yes," agreed the other, "that house will never stand up to the strong winter winds. It will let the rain in and, what's more, it won't protect you from the big bad wolf." The lazy little pig brushed his brothers' worries aside with a wave of his hand and ran off to play.

The second little pig was determined to build a stronger, safer house than his brother, and sat down to think about what he would use. But he soon became distracted by the sight of his brother having such fun, so he built himself a house as quickly as possible so that he could join in. The second little pig gathered together as many bundles of sticks as he could find and built them up into a house.

The last little pig looked at this and shook his head. But the second little pig took no notice and ran off to join his brother playing in the field. The last little pig set about building his own house. He spent a long time building it from bricks and cement, and ignored his brothers' pleas to join them at play. Finally, the house of bricks was finished, and the third little pig was very proud of himself.

One day soon after the third house was completed, the wolf was prowling around the neighborhood, and he was very

hungry. He soon came upon the first little pig's house made of straw. His stomach began to rumble, and he called out in his deep, growly voice, "Little pig, little pig, let me come in."

The poor little pig was very frightened. He knew that the wolf wanted to have him for his dinner. He called back in a trembling voice, "No, Mr. Wolf. Not by the hair on my chinny-chin-chin!"

"Very well," snarled the horrible wolf, "then I'll huff, and I'll puff, and I'll blow your house down!" He took a deep breath, puffed out his cheeks, and blew as hard as he could. Sure enough, the house of straw could not stand up to the power of the wolf. Clouds of straw flew all over the place, and the house fell to the ground, leaving the little pig with no shelter. He ran as fast as he could to his brother's house of sticks and hammered on the door.

The wolf soon came to the house of sticks and could hear the scared voices of the two little pigs who were inside. "Little pigs, little pigs, let me come in," he called again.

"No, Mr. Wolf," came the reply. "Not by the hair on our chinny-chin-chins!"

The wolf licked his lips. "Very well, then I'll huff, and I'll puff, and I'll blow your house down!" He blew and blew, and

very soon the house of sticks began to shake and wobble. Before too long, it tumbled down around the terrified little pigs, who were huddled together in fear.

Puffing and panting, they ran to their brother's house of bricks, shouting, "Help us. The wolf is coming!"

The third little pig heard their cries and opened his door wide to let them in. "Don't be afraid," he told them. "This house will never fall down."

The wolf prowled around the house of bricks. His mouth watered at the thought of the three little pigs trapped inside. "Little pigs, little pigs, let me come in," he called again, and he was not surprised to hear three voices shout, "No!" from inside the house.

The wolf smiled and began huffing and puffing, trying to blow down the house of bricks. As hard as he tried, the house would not budge. He realized that he would have to try something else if he wanted to get inside. He scrambled up onto the roof of the house, thinking that he would climb down the chimney. The pigs heard the wolf scrabbling and scratching above their heads and knew what he was up to.

"I have a plan," said the third little pig. "We must light the fire right away."

Soon they had a crackling fire burning. They could hear the wolf coming down the chimney, and they knew their plan had worked. With a loud thump, the wolf landed in the fireplace. His tail caught on fire, and he ran howling from the house. He knew when he was beaten and vowed never to trouble the pigs again. The two lazy pigs had learned their lessons, too. They built their own houses of bricks so that they would always be safe.

Crow Brings Daylight
(A story from the Pacific Northwest)

A very long time ago, in the lands of the far north where it is icy and cold, darkness reigned, and it was always night. The people of the north had never seen the sun, but they did not mind. In fact, they thought that the whole world was as dark as their black lands.

One day, an old crow, who often traveled far from the lands of the north, came back from one of his journeys full of stories about the Daylight. He spoke of how it filled the sky with light and the world with color. The people of the north, sitting around their campfires, were amazed by Crow's tales. Soon, news of the Daylight and its wondrous power had spread throughout the cold, dark land.

Everyone wanted to see this marvelous thing, and they all realized how useful it would be. "Think how much easier it would be for us to hunt," said one man.

"Crow," said the people of the north, "you must go and fetch us this Daylight, for you are the only one who knows where to find it." Crow protested that he was too old to fly so far, but the people kept asking him. Eventually he agreed.

Off he went into the dark sky, flapping his wings as fast as he could. He flew for a very long time, until he grew so tired that he almost turned back to fly home again. Then, suddenly, he caught sight of the glow of the Daylight in the distance, and he knew that he had almost reached his destination. He fluttered his tired black wings with all his strength and flew toward the glimmering light. He smiled with pleasure as it got brighter and brighter, filling the sky.

Soon, Crow came to a village that was on the banks of a wide river. He landed in a tree to rest, marveling at how blue the sky had turned because of the Daylight.

A beautiful woman came to fetch water from the icy river. The old crow could tell from the fine furs she was wearing that she was the daughter of the chief of the village. The crafty bird turned himself into a speck of dust and floated down toward the woman. He settled on her cloak and was carried with her as she returned to the lodge where her father lived.

When he got inside, Crow saw the chief's little grandson playing on the floor. As the woman took off her cloak, Crow floated over to the child and landed in his ear, scratching him a little and making him cry out. The chief of the village loved all of his children and grandchildren dearly, but this little boy was his favorite, and he couldn't bear to see him upset or sad. Right away, he ran to the child, asking, "What's wrong? Whatever is the matter?"

"Tell him you want to play with a ball of Daylight," whispered Crow inside the boy's ear. The little boy pointed at a glowing box high up on a shelf and told his grandfather that he wanted to play with what was inside. The chief told his daughter to fetch the box from the shelf. When it was opened, Crow gasped to see many balls of Daylight shining and sparkling inside.

The chief took one small ball from the box, tied a string around it, and gave it to his grandson. The child laughed with delight and bounced it happily on the floor, watching the colors change inside it.

After a few moments, Crow scratched at the boy's ear once more, and tears began running down the boy's face. "Why are you crying, my boy?" asked

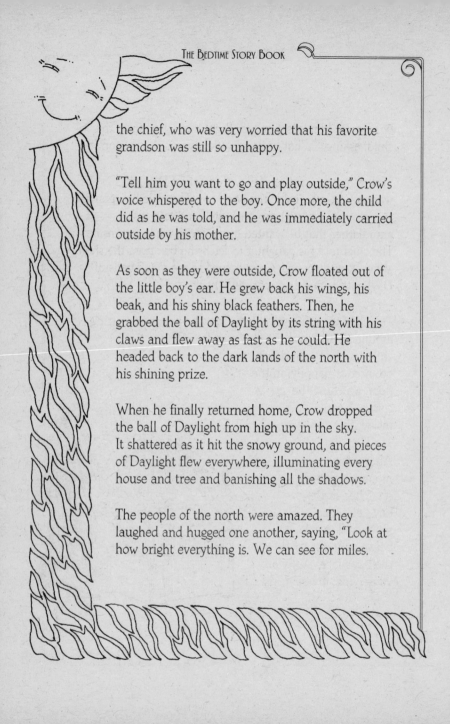

the chief, who was very worried that his favorite grandson was still so unhappy.

"Tell him you want to go and play outside," Crow's voice whispered to the boy. Once more, the child did as he was told, and he was immediately carried outside by his mother.

As soon as they were outside, Crow floated out of the little boy's ear. He grew back his wings, his beak, and his shiny black feathers. Then, he grabbed the ball of Daylight by its string with his claws and flew away as fast as he could. He headed back to the dark lands of the north with his shining prize.

When he finally returned home, Crow dropped the ball of Daylight from high up in the sky. It shattered as it hit the snowy ground, and pieces of Daylight flew everywhere, illuminating every house and tree and banishing all the shadows.

The people of the north were amazed. They laughed and hugged one another, saying, "Look at how bright everything is. We can see for miles.

Thank you, Crow. Thank you for bringing us the wonderful Daylight."

"I am only small," replied Crow. "I could carry only one tiny ball of Daylight, and it will need to regain its strength from time to time. You will be able to live in Daylight for only half of the year, and for the other half you will be in darkness as before. I am sorry."

The people of the north did not mind one bit. "We are so happy to have the Daylight at all. If it had not been for you, we would still have been living every day in darkness and shadow."

They were so happy with this arrangement that it has always remained. Even now, the north lands are light for half of the year and dark for the other half. The people have not forgotten that it was Crow who brought them the Daylight, and they treat all of his grandchildren and great grandchildren with kindness and respect because of it.

City Mouse and
Country Mouse
(Adapted from the fable by Aesop)

Once upon a time, there were two mice who were very great
friends. One of them, with soft brown fur and a long tail,
lived in the countryside. He loved scampering around the
fields in the sunshine. The other was gray, with beady black
eyes, and he lived in the pantry of a tall house in the city.

One day, the city mouse decided to visit his friend in the
country. The country mouse was very pleased to see him
and welcomed his friend into his little home, which was in
the middle of a field of golden corn. The country mouse had
spent a long time preparing a meal for the city mouse's
visit, and his table was groaning under the weight of all the
grain, nuts, and berries that he had gathered.

The city mouse was very shocked when he saw this food.
"Oh!" he said. "How on earth do you survive with only this
sort of food to eat? You must come and stay with me right
this instant, and I will show you what you are missing."
Together, the two friends set off for the city. They traveled
for many hours, singing songs and telling jokes. By the time
they reached the city mouse's house, it was dinnertime,
and they were both very hungry.

The city mouse scuttled into the tall town house and proudly showed his friend around his home, pointing out each of the delicious things to eat as they ran happily around the shelves of the pantry. The country mouse couldn't believe his eyes—everywhere he looked there was something new and tasty to nibble at. There were huge cheeses, legs of ham, jars of honey, jams, chutneys, breads, and cakes that he couldn't wait to try.

The two friends dug into their feast and munched away happily in silence. Just as the little country mouse was about to bite into a particularly tasty piece of cheese, there was a deafening sound of barking. The country mouse squeaked with fear and ran, shaking and trembling, to his friend.

"Don't worry, my friend," said the city mouse calmly. "It's only the

family's dog." The country mouse
took a deep breath and tried to stop his heart
from beating too fast as he went back to his meal.

After a while, both mice began to feel very full.
They were looking forward to relaxing after all
their eating. Suddenly, they heard scratching
at the pantry door, and through a crack in the
wood they could see two glowing yellow eyes. This
time it was the city mouse who was nervous. "Run
for it!" he squeaked. "That's the house cat, and
she'll want us for her dinner if she finds us."

As fast as they could, they scampered into a hole in the
baseboard and stayed there, trying not to make a sound.
Their little hiding place was cramped and uncomfortable,
and the country mouse was feeling fed up. He was hot,
frightened, and his stomach hurt. As soon as the cat had
stopped prowling around outside the pantry and
gone off to find food, the country mouse
thanked his friend for his kindness
and went to the door to begin his
journey home.

"You're not leaving already,
are you?" asked the city
mouse, who was hungry

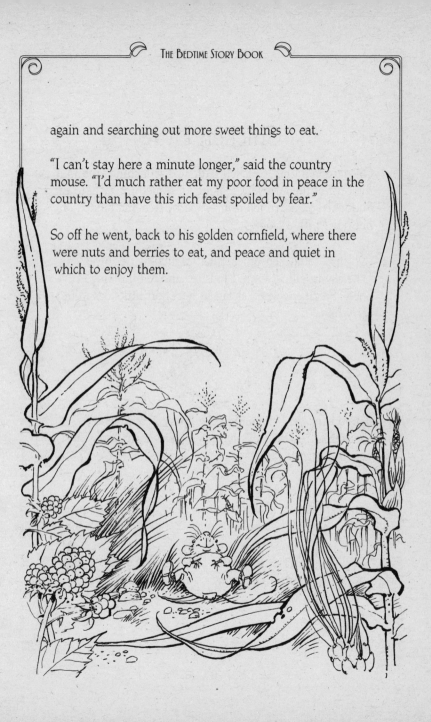

again and searching out more sweet things to eat.

"I can't stay here a minute longer," said the country mouse. "I'd much rather eat my poor food in peace in the country than have this rich feast spoiled by fear."

So off he went, back to his golden cornfield, where there were nuts and berries to eat, and peace and quiet in which to enjoy them.

Chicken Little

Once upon a time, Chicken Little was scratching around in the dust of the farmyard looking for something tasty to eat. Suddenly, an acorn fell from a nearby tree and landed on her head with a *clonk*.

"Oh my!" squawked Chicken Little, rubbing her head. "The sky is falling down. I must go and tell the king at once." So off she went, as fast as her short little legs would carry her.

Before very long, she met Cocky Locky. "Hello there, Chicken Little," said Cocky Locky. "Where are you going on this fine day?"

"It is not a fine day at all, Cocky Locky. The sky is falling down. A piece of it hit me on my head, and I am going to tell the king."

"Goodness, Chicken Little, that does sound serious," said Cocky Locky, frowning. "May I come with you?"

"Of course you may," said Chicken Little to Cocky Locky, and off they went to see the king and tell him that the sky was falling.

They had not gotten very far when they met Ducky Lucky, who was splashing around in a pond.

"Hello there, you two," said Ducky Lucky to Chicken Little and Cocky Locky. "Where are you going in such a hurry?"

"Oh, Ducky Lucky," said Cocky Locky, "the sky is falling down. A piece of it hit Chicken Little on the head, so we are going to tell the king."

Ducky Lucky flapped her wings in surprise when she heard this news. "How awful," she said in a worried voice. "May I come with you to tell the king, Chicken Little?"

"Of course you may," said Chicken Little, and so Ducky Lucky got out of the pond and joined Chicken Little and Cocky Locky on their way to see the king. Very soon, the three travelers spied Goosey Lucy waddling toward them on the path. "Goosey Lucy," called out Ducky Lucky as soon as she saw her friend. "You must come quickly; the sky is falling down."

"Yes," said Chicken Little, "a piece of it fell on my head. We are going to tell the king."

"Good heavens!" cried Goosey Lucy. "I would like to come with you to tell the king about that."

"Of course, Goosey Lucy, the more the merrier," said Cocky Locky, patting her on the back. Chicken Little now had quite a procession following her on her way to see the king, and soon enough there was one more. Turkey Lurkey was clucking and gobbling to himself when he saw his friends pass him, all walking and waddling very fast.

"Hello there, everyone. Where are you all rushing off to?" Turkey Lurkey called after them. Chicken Little, Cocky Locky, Ducky Lucky, and Goosey Lucy turned their heads and called back, all at the same time, "The sky is falling. We are going to tell the king."

Turkey Lurkey gasped when he heard this. "This is terrible," he said. "Wait. Let me come with you." And off he ran to catch up with the others.

After a while, Chicken Little, Cocky Locky, Ducky Lucky, Goosey Lucy, and Turkey Lurkey came to a big forest full of tall trees. As they would soon find out, it was in these woods that Foxy Loxy lived.

Foxy Loxy saw the group of travelers coming toward him through the woods, and he stepped out from behind a tree into their path. "Well, well, what have we here?" he said, in his smooth, syrupy voice.

"Oh!" said Chicken Little, who was a bit startled. "Hello there, Foxy Loxy. The most terrible thing has happened. A piece of the sky fell on my head, and we are going to tell the king about it."

A smile spread over Foxy Loxy's sly face when he heard this. "Yes, you must tell the king right away," he said. "Come with me. I know a shortcut that will get you to the palace much faster." Chicken Little, Cocky Locky, Ducky Lucky, Goosey Lucy, and Turkey Lurkey were very grateful for Foxy Loxy's help. They followed him through the trees, as he led them deeper and deeper into the woods.

Soon, they came to the entrance of a cave. "If you go through this tunnel, you will come out right next to the palace, and you will be able to tell the king about the sky falling down," said Foxy Loxy. Chicken Little, Cocky Locky, Ducky Lucky, Goosey Lucy, and Turkey Lurkey thanked him and went inside. Foxy Loxy licked his lips with his pink tongue and followed them into the cave.

By the time Chicken Little and her friends realized that they had been tricked, it was too late. The king was never told that the sky was falling down, and the only one to come out of the cave a few days later was a very full and very fat Foxy Loxy.

Anansi and the Sky God
(A story from Africa)

A very long time ago, there were no stories on earth;
no one had any tales to tell. There were no beginnings
and no endings. All the stories were kept in a great, carved
wooden box under the throne of Nyame, the Sky God, who
lived high above the clouds.

The spider Anansi, who made his home in Africa and
spun his silvery webs between the tall trees, wanted the
stories for himself. One day, he made a ladder from silken
thread and climbed into the heavens to see the Sky God
and ask for the stories he kept locked away.

When Nyame heard the spider's request, he smiled.
"Anansi," he said, in his deep, rumbling voice, "you are not
the first to come here and ask me for my stories. I will not
just give them away, and the price I ask for them is high."

"I will do whatever you ask," said the spider.

"My price is this: You must bring me Mmboro, the tribe of hornets; Onini, the terrible python who swallows men whole; Osebo, the leopard with his sharp, sharp teeth; and Mmoatia, the fairy, who is almost never seen. Many have tried to do this, Anansi, but no one has succeeded."

The spider turned and left the palace of the Sky God. He promised to bring Nyame everything that he had asked for. "First," he thought, "I must capture Mmboro, the hornets with the fearsome stings." He fetched a gourd and made a small hole in it; then he dipped a bowl into a nearby stream and took both of these things to the great, old tree where the hornets lived. Anansi poured some of the water from the bowl over himself and threw the rest of it onto the hornets' hive.

"Quick!" he called out. "Mmboro, the rain is falling. Fly into this dry gourd so that the water doesn't damage your wings."

A stream of hornets flew into the gourd that Anansi held out to them and buzzed their thanks to the spider. Quick as a flash, Anansi plugged the hole in the gourd with some

banana leaves, leaving the angry hornets trapped inside. "Fools," said the spider. "I am taking you to Nyame, the Sky God."

When Nyame saw that the hornets had been successfully captured, he nodded and said, "Good, Anansi, but three tasks remain."

Anansi set about his next task—trapping Onini, the enormous python. Onini was a clever beast, and Anansi knew that he would need some help coming up with a plan. So, he went to his wife, Aso, and asked for her advice.

"Onini is clever, it is true, but he is also vain," she said, and she whispered her plan into Anansi's ear. Right away, the spider cut a long branch from a nearby palm tree, and some long, thick vines. He took these to the riverbank where Onini lived. As he approached the rushing river, he began talking loudly to himself. "I am right, I know it. I say he is long and strong. How can my wife think as she does? I do not understand her—she is wrong; she is definitely wrong."

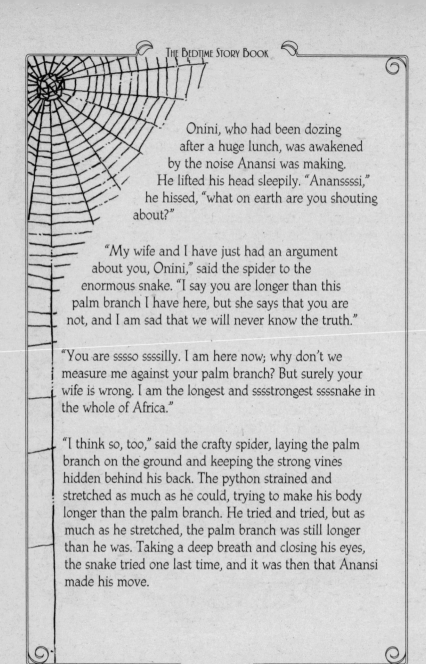

Onini, who had been dozing after a huge lunch, was awakened by the noise Anansi was making. He lifted his head sleepily. "Anansssi," he hissed, "what on earth are you shouting about?"

"My wife and I have just had an argument about you, Onini," said the spider to the enormous snake. "I say you are longer than this palm branch I have here, but she says that you are not, and I am sad that we will never know the truth."

"You are sssso ssssilly. I am here now; why don't we measure me against your palm branch? But surely your wife is wrong. I am the longest and sssstrongest ssssnake in the whole of Africa."

"I think so, too," said the crafty spider, laying the palm branch on the ground and keeping the strong vines hidden behind his back. The python strained and stretched as much as he could, trying to make his body longer than the palm branch. He tried and tried, but as much as he stretched, the palm branch was still longer than he was. Taking a deep breath and closing his eyes, the snake tried one last time, and it was then that Anansi made his move.

He quickly tied the snake's head to one end of the branch with a vine, and his tail to the other, so that he could not escape. Then, using the rest of the vines, Anansi bound the snake tightly to the branch and carried him up to the clouds to present him to the Sky God.

Next on the spider's list was Osebo, the leopard, whose growling voice could often be heard echoing through the jungle. Late at night, Anansi dug a deep hole in the ground, where he knew Osebo often went walking. He covered it with sticks and leaves until it was completely hidden. Then he crept into the bushes and waited for the leopard to arrive. Early in the morning, he heard Osebo's padding footsteps approaching, and, sure enough, Osebo fell with a yelp straight into Anansi's trap.

The spider scuttled over to the edge of the pit and looked in at the leopard lying on the floor. "Why, Osebo," he said, "how on earth did this happen to you?"

Osebo's green eyes flashed with anger. "I have fallen into a trap. You must help me out, Spider," he said rudely.

Anansi bent a young, green tree over toward the ground and tied it so that the top branches were hovering over the pit. Then he tied another rope to the top of the tree and let it dangle down into the hole below.

"Here you are, Osebo. Tie the end of this rope to your tail, and I will pull you out."

The leopard did as he was told. Anansi burst out laughing and cut the rope that was holding the tree to the ground. It sprang back into shape, hauling the snarling leopard out of the hole and leaving him hanging by his tail, helpless above the ground. The clever spider climbed up the trunk and spun a huge web around his prey. "Come with me, Osebo," he said with a smile on his face. "We are going to meet the Sky God."

Nyame nodded once again when he saw the leopard struggling in Anansi's web. "Good, Anansi," he said. "Now, bring me Mmoatia, and your task will be complete."

Anansi knew that to see the tiny fairy Mmoatia was very rare, and that to catch her was almost impossible. He had heard many stories of how much she loved to play, and so the sneaky spider came up with a plan.

He carved a small doll out of wood and placed it near a pool where the fairy liked to come and play in the cool water. He smeared the doll with the sticky sap from a nearby tree and, at its feet, he put a bowl of tasty yams. Soon, the beautiful fairy came fluttering to the pool, and she spied the bowl of yams right away.

"May I please share your yams?" she asked the doll, in a voice that sounded like little bells ringing. Of course, the wooden doll did not say anything in reply.

The fairy tried again. "I would like to eat some yams. May I?" Still there was no answer. After a while, Mmoatia grew angry. She flew at the doll in a rage, hitting and kicking it. But, as soon as her hands and feet touched the wood of the doll, she stuck to the sap that was covering it and could not get free.

Anansi scuttled out from his hiding place and picked up the doll and the furious fairy. Laughing softly to himself, he took her to the Sky God as his prisoner. Nyame was shocked that the spider had done everything that he asked, but he was a man of his word. He held out the wooden box of stories to Anansi.

"Congratulations, my friend. These stories belong to you. From now on, we will call them Spider Stories so that the world knows of your success."

Little Red Riding Hood

(Adapted from the story by The Brothers Grimm)

In a cottage at the edge of a forest, there lived a little girl and her mother. Everyone who knew the little girl was very fond of her, and they named her Little Red Riding Hood because of the red velvet cape and hood she loved to wear.

One day, her mother gave her a basket filled with cakes and bread. She told her to take it through the woods to her grandmother's cottage. "Grandma is weak and has been ill. These cakes will make her feel better," she said. "Go straight to her cottage, Little Red Riding Hood. Don't dawdle in the woods, and don't stray from the path."

"Don't worry, Mother," said Little Red Riding Hood. "I will run straight to Grandma's house to give her these delicious cakes." She carried the basket on her arm and skipped off along the path and into the woods.

Her grandmother lived in a small cottage with a thatched roof, right at the end of the path. Little Red Riding Hood had to go deep into the woods to get there, but the sun was shining and the birds were singing. She smiled happily, enjoying the scenery as she walked. Unbeknownst to Little Red Riding Hood, someone was watching her walk along the path, someone with big yellow eyes and sharp teeth — the wolf.

After a while, the sly old wolf decided it was time to introduce himself to the girl. He stepped out from behind a tree and padded alongside her. "Hello there," he said in a gruff voice. "Where is a pretty young thing like you going on this fine day?"

"Hello there, Mr. Wolf," said Little Red Riding Hood, sweetly. "I am going to take these cakes to my grandmother, who has been ill."

"How lovely," said the wolf, baring his teeth in a grin. "Tell me, child, where does your grandmother live?"

The little girl did not know that wolves are cunning creatures, always looking for their next meal, nor did she see the wolf licking his lips hungrily. She simply replied to his question honestly, telling him that Grandma lived in the little thatched cottage underneath the great old oak tree at the end of the path. "If I am clever," thought the wolf to himself, "I will be able to have the old woman and her tender young granddaughter for my dinner."

Out loud, he said, "Look at all these beautiful flowers blooming today. Don't you think your grandmother would like a pretty bouquet to brighten up her room?"

Little Red Riding Hood remembered the promise she had made to her mother, but she couldn't help agreeing with the wolf. The flowers were beautiful, and she felt sure her grandmother would be cheered by a few bunches of the brightest ones she could find.

"What a good idea, Mr. Wolf. How clever you are," she said, and skipped off the path and among the trees to begin picking flowers.

The wolf felt very pleased with himself. As soon as the little red cape was out of sight, he scampered down the path to the old woman's house and knocked on the door.

"Who's there?" Grandma called out in a shaky voice.

The wolf did his best to make his voice sound high and childlike. "It is Little Red Riding Hood. I have brought you some cakes to make you feel better."

"Lift the latch and come in, my dear," said the old woman.

No sooner were the words out of her mouth than the hungry wolf had bounded into the cottage and swallowed her whole. Then he put on her cap and her shawl and climbed into bed to wait for Little Red Riding Hood.

By this time, the little girl had gathered a wonderful bunch of red and yellow flowers. She tied them together with a ribbon from her hair and hurried on to her grandmother's house to present her with her gifts.

When the wolf heard the knock on the door, he answered in a shaky voice, "Who's there?"

"It is Little Red Riding Hood, Grandma. I have come with some presents for you."

"Lift the latch and come in, dear," said the crafty wolf.

The little girl came into the cottage, put the basket down, and stared at her grandmother, lying in the bed.

"Why, Grandma, what big ears you have," she said, suddenly feeling a little uneasy.

"All the better to hear you with, my dear," said the wolf, trying to keep the growl out of his voice.

"And what big eyes you have, Grandma."

"All the better to see you with."

"What big hands you have."

"All the better to hug you with, little one."

"And what big teeth you have, Grandma."

"All the better to eat you with!" The wolf threw back the
blankets and leaped upon the little girl, gobbling her up
in one mouthful. Feeling drowsy after his enormous dinner,
the wolf got back into bed and fell into a deep, deep sleep.

A little later, a hunter was passing by the cottage under the
great oak tree. He had heard that the old woman who lived
there had been ill and wanted to give her his best wishes
for a speedy recovery. When he peeped in the window
and saw the greedy wolf asleep in her bed, he guessed
immediately what must have happened. He ran into the
house as fast as he could.

The hunter pointed his gun at the fat stomach of the sleeping wolf. He was about to pull the trigger when he realized that the old woman might possibly still be alive inside the wolf. The hunter knew how greedy the horrible creature was, and thought he might well have swallowed her whole. Taking a pair of scissors, he started snipping away at the wolf's furry stomach. The beast was so deeply asleep that he didn't even stir. Soon, the hunter had cut open the whole stomach. To his amazement, out popped not only the old woman, but also her little granddaughter. Both were frightened, but neither was hurt. They hugged each other with joy.

"Oh, thank you, sir," they both said. "What would we have done without you?"

The three of them gathered up some large stones and filled the sleeping wolf's stomach with them. Then they sewed his stomach back together and tiptoed from the house. The hunter took his gun and fired a loud shot up into the air, waking up the wolf with a start. The wolf bounded out of bed, but the stones in his stomach were so heavy that he fell to the floor and died.

Grandma was able to enjoy her cakes in peace, and Little Red Riding Hood promised that she would never again stray from the path.

The Three Billy Goats Gruff
(A story from Norway)

There were once three billy goats, and each one had the name Gruff, because of his rough, bleating voice and the tufts of hair that grew from his chin. They had spent the winter eating straw and hay in the barn that they lived in to keep warm, but now the snows were melting. The sun was shining, and everything was green again. The three hungry billy goats decided to go into the mountains to eat the sweet, green grass that grew there.

To get to the mountains, they had to cross a rickety wooden bridge over a rushing river. Now, under this bridge lived an ugly troll, with bulging eyes, huge claws,

and a terrible temper. Everyone was terrified of him
and never crossed the bridge in case he tried to gobble
them up.

The three billy goats Gruff had heard of this troll and,
although they were scared, they were also very hungry.
They simply could not wait to eat some of the
delicious mountain grass. So, they decided to take
a risk and cross the old bridge.

The littlest billy goat was the first
to reach the bridge, and he trotted over
it. *Trip, trap, trip, trap* went his little hooves
upon the wooden planks. Suddenly, the troll's
ugly head popped up from underneath the bridge.
"Who dares to cross over my bridge?" he roared
angrily.

"I am a billy goat Gruff," said the littlest billy
goat. "I am going to the mountains to graze on
the grass."

"Oh no, you are not," yelled the troll. "You are going to be my dinner. I am starving, and a tasty billy goat is just what I need."

The littlest billy goat's knees began to tremble. "Please, Mr. Troll, don't eat me. I am the smallest and skinniest of the billy goats Gruff; I would not be a very satisfying meal for you. It would be better for you if you waited for my brother — he is much bigger and will be much tastier."

The troll thought about this for a while and decided that the littlest billy goat was probably right. He was very hungry after all, and he did not want to waste his appetite on such a small meal. "Very well," he growled, "you may cross my bridge." The little billy goat trotted happily over the bridge, and off he went into the mountains.

Soon enough, the middle-size billy goat Gruff came to cross the bridge. His hooves had hardly started trip-trapping across before he came face-to-face with the horrible troll. The poor billy goat did not need to be told that the troll was looking for a meal — he could hear a loud rumbling and gurgling coming from the creature's stomach. "Who dares to cross my bridge?" shouted the troll.

"I am a billy goat Gruff," said the medium-size billy goat. "I am going to fill my stomach with grass in the mountains."

"You are mistaken," growled the troll. "I am going to fill my stomach with you. You are going to be my dinner."

The poor billy goat bleated with fear. "Please, Mr. Troll, don't eat me," he said. "My brother is on his way, and he is much bigger and fatter than I am. Eat him instead — he will fill you up much more than I will."

Again, the troll pondered this for a while, and eventually he decided that he was definitely hungry enough to eat a really big billy goat, not just a medium-size one. So, the second billy goat was allowed to cross over the bridge and go up into the mountains to find his little brother.

After a while, the biggest billy goat came trip-trapping over the bridge. He was so big that the noise of his hooves made the bridge start to shake. He had not gotten far across the bridge when the troll reared his ugly head. "Who dares cross my bridge?"

"I am a billy goat Gruff," replied the biggest billy goat. "I am going into the mountains to eat my fill of lovely grass."

"Not so fast, Billy Goat Gruff," shouted the angry troll. "I am so hungry, and you are going to be my dinner. I am going to eat you up right this instant."

"Is that what you think, Mr. Troll?" said the billy goat with a smile. He ran at the troll as fast as he could and butted the huge creature over the side of the bridge.

The troll fell far, far down through the air and landed with a splash in the river below. The current of the river was strong, and the troll could not swim. The biggest billy goat watched as the horrible troll was carried far away in the rushing water. Then he trip-trapped across the bridge and into the mountains to find his brothers. From that day onward, everyone was free to cross the bridge in peace.

Cap o' Rushes
(A story from the British Isles)

Long ago, there lived a very rich gentleman who had three beautiful daughters. He loved each of them very much and was always showering them with gifts. They had fine clothes to wear and delicious food to eat, and they never went without anything that they wanted.

One day, the rich man decided to see how much his daughters loved him. He called his eldest daughter to him. "My darling daughter," he said, "how much do you love your old father?"

The girl answered without a moment's hesitation. "Father, I love you as much as the sun, the moon, and the stars." The old man was very satisfied indeed with this answer. He patted his daughter's golden curls and sent her on her way.

Next, he called for his second daughter. "My darling daughter," he asked once again, "how much do you love your old father?"

Again, the reply came back right away. "Why, Father, I love you as much as my own life." The girl's father hugged her and smiled. This, too, was an answer that made him very happy.

Then, he called for his youngest daughter, who was even more beautiful than her two lovely sisters. For a third time, the rich man asked how much his daughter loved him.

There was a silence. The young girl thought long and hard about how to answer her father's question, and she bit her lip in concentration. After a while, her eyes lit up, and she said, "Father, I love you as much as meat loves salt."

Her father grew angry when he heard this. "You ungrateful child. You do not love me at all!" he shouted in a rage. He marched her to the front door. "Leave my house at once and never return," he yelled, and slammed the door in her face.

The poor girl had nothing apart from the elegant dress she wore. She walked for many miles, with tears streaming down her face, until she came to a lake, by the side of which grew many long rushes.

She gathered great armfuls of them and wove them together until she had made a cloak of rushes with a hood. She slipped her new cloak over her dress so that her fine clothes would be hidden from sight. Anyone who saw her would think she was nothing more than a simple peasant woman.

Then, the unfortunate young girl continued her journey, until she came to a large mansion. She knocked on the door and asked the kind-looking maid who answered if she might find some work to do in the house. "Please," she said, "I'll be no trouble. I have nowhere to go, and I'll do any jobs that need doing in return for a place to sleep and a little food."

The housekeeper at the mansion liked how polite the young girl was. She agreed to let her sleep in the servants' quarters and share their food, and set her to work scrubbing the dirty pots and pans. The girl would not tell anyone her name, so the servants in the mansion called her Cap o' Rushes, because of the hooded cloak that she always wore.

One day, the servants were all very excited because there was to be a grand ball held at the mansion that night. Lots of elegant young men and beautiful young women from all over the land had been invited. When evening came, the servants all went to watch the grand people arriving in their carriages. Cap o' Rushes said that she was too tired to go with them. But, once they had all gone, she slipped off her cloak and hood and, dressed in her fine clothes, sneaked into the ballroom.

She was the most beautiful woman in the room, and the young master of the house fell in love with her as soon as he saw her. He refused to dance with anyone else for the whole night.

Just before midnight, Cap o' Rushes slipped away from the ballroom and ran back to the servants' quarters. By the time the other maids came back, she was fast asleep, dressed once more in her cloak of rushes.

The next day, everyone was gossiping about the ball and the mysterious beautiful woman off whom the young master had not been able to take his eyes. No one knew who she was, but they all agreed that she was the most beautiful woman they had ever seen.

"I wish I could have seen her," said Cap o' Rushes, and she smiled to herself.

Not long afterward, it was announced that there would be another ball at the mansion. Again, the servants went off to watch everyone arriving and again, Cap o' Rushes pretended she was too tired to join them. However, when they had gone, she slipped off her cloak and rushed to the ballroom to dance with the young master again. He asked her her name, but she only smiled and said nothing. The young master gave her a ring and told her that if he didn't see her again, he would die of heartbreak. Once again, Cap o' Rushes left the ball before it was over, ran back to her bed, and slipped on her peasant woman's cloak and her hood.

For many days after the ball, the young master tried to find out the identity of the mystery lady. When he could

not, he grew tired and weak and went to bed, suffering
terribly from lovesickness.

The cook was very worried about the master's health,
and she made him a large bowl of gruel every day to help
him get his strength back. One day, Cap o' Rushes asked
the cook if she could make the master's gruel that day. The
cook was fond of the young girl and agreed to let her help.
When no one was looking, Cap o' Rushes slipped the ring
that the master had given her into the bowl of gruel and
gave it to a maid to take up to him in his bedroom.

When the master saw the ring lying at the bottom of the
bowl, he grew very excited and sent for the cook
immediately. "Who made this gruel?" he demanded.

"It was Cap o' Rushes who made it," said the cook.

"Send Cap o' Rushes to me at once," the young man said,
sitting up straight in his bed.

When Cap o' Rushes arrived, he asked her right away where she had gotten the ring that was in his bowl of gruel. The girl's face lit up in a beautiful smile.

"I got this ring from you, sir," she replied. She took off her cloak and her hood and stood before him as the beautiful woman he had danced with at the ball.

The young master was overjoyed and vowed that they would be married before the end of the week. All the rich noblemen and -women from all over the land were invited to the wedding, including Cap o' Rushes's father, who she had not seen for many months.

Before the wedding, Cap o' Rushes went to her friend the cook and told her to prepare every dish without salt.

"But, ma'am"—for this is how the servants addressed her now that she was going to become their mistress—"without salt, the food will have no flavor—it will taste horrible."

"I know." Cap o' Rushes smiled. "But please, do as I say."

The wedding day came, and, after the sweethearts were married, the guests sat down to the great wedding feast, which did not contain a single grain of salt. Everyone complained at how tasteless the food was. Many refused to eat more than a few mouthfuls. One guest, though, tried each and every dish and then burst into loud sobs.

"Sir, what is the matter?" asked the other guests. Cap o' Rushes's father dried his eyes and told them about the day he had asked his daughters how much they loved him.

"I thought my youngest girl did not love me because she said that she loved me as much as meat loves salt, and I threw her out of my house. Now I see that she really did love me very much, and I don't know where she is."

Cap o' Rushes ran to her father and hugged him. "Father, I am here. I am safe, and I forgive you," she cried. Everyone laughed with joy, and the rich gentleman welcomed his new son-in-law into his family.

The Goose Girl
(Adapted from the story by The Brothers Grimm)

Once upon a time, there was an old, widowed queen who had a beautiful daughter. When she was a little girl, the princess was betrothed to a young prince in a faraway kingdom. She lived a happy and pleasant life with her mother and grew into a lovely young woman.

Soon, the time came for her to be married, and she had to make the long journey from her palace to the kingdom of her future husband. The old queen was very sad to see her daughter leaving, for she loved her with all her heart.

The queen made sure that her daughter would have everything she could possibly want on her long journey. She sent her away with many golden and silver trinkets, strings of pearls, and other fine jewels. The queen also gave her daughter a maid to ride with her and make sure that she was always safe and comfortable, and a loyal old horse named Falada, who had the magical gift of speech.

When it came time for mother and daughter to say good-bye, the old queen gave her daughter one last gift. She handed her a handkerchief with three drops of her own blood on it. "Take this, my dear child. Keep it hidden away. It will be useful to you on your journey."

The young princess did as she was told, and she tucked the handkerchief into her dress. Then she hugged her mother, weeping with sadness, before mounting her horse and riding off toward her bridegroom in his distant palace.

After a long while, the young princess felt very thirsty. She asked her maid, who was riding next to her, to fetch her a goblet of water from a nearby stream.

"I will do no such thing," replied the maid haughtily. "You can dismount from your horse and get a drink yourself. I do not wish to be your servant."

The princess felt saddened by the maid's rudeness, but she was so thirsty that she did as she was told. She got down from her horse, bent down over the stream, and drank the cool water. She sighed with unhappiness. To her

amazement, the three drops of blood on her handkerchief answered, "If your mother knew, her heart would break in two."

On they rode again for many more miles, until the princess once again felt that her throat was parched from thirst. "Please," she said politely to her maid, "will you fetch me my golden cup and take it to the stream there so that I may have a drink?"

"If you want a drink, you can fetch it for yourself," replied the maid, even more rudely than before. "I do not choose to be your servant."

Again, the princess was forced to go to the stream and lie down to drink. This time, two tears ran down her face, and again the drops of blood said, "If your mother knew, her heart would break in two."

As the princess was bending over the rushing water, the handkerchief fell from her dress and floated away down the stream. She was so troubled by her situation that she did not even notice it, but the maid certainly did. The cruel maid smiled with glee because she knew that without the handkerchief, the princess would be powerless and weak.

When the princess returned from the stream, she saw that her maid was sitting upon Falada. "This horse is mine now," she said. "You will have to ride my old nag." Then the maid forced the princess to swap clothes with her, making her give away all her finery. "You must not tell a soul about this," said the maid threateningly. "If you do, I swear that you will be killed." Falada, the loyal horse, saw all of this, and his heart filled with sadness for his mistress.

The poor princess had no choice but to do as she was told. As they approached the royal palace where the prince lived, everyone at his court thought that the maid was the princess and that the princess was the maid. The prince lifted the false bride from her horse and embraced her, a beaming smile on his face. The cruel maid was escorted into the palace with much cheering and rejoicing, and the princess was left standing alone in the courtyard.

A while later, the old king happened to look out of the window and saw the beautiful young woman staring forlornly up at the palace. He was struck by how pretty she was, and he asked the bride-to-be who she was.

"Oh, she's no one important," sneered the false princess. "Just a maid I brought with me to help me on my journey. Please find her some work to do—she's an idle creature."

The king thought about this for a while. "There is a young boy who tends the geese—she can assist him with his duties," he said. The prince's bride-to-be seemed very pleased indeed with this.

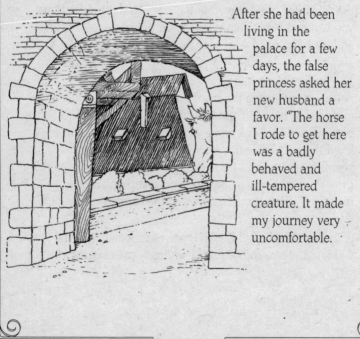

After she had been living in the palace for a few days, the false princess asked her new husband a favor. "The horse I rode to get here was a badly behaved and ill-tempered creature. It made my journey very uncomfortable.

Please, dearest husband, cut off its head."

Poor Falada had, of course, done nothing wrong, but the maid knew of his ability to speak and was worried that he might reveal her terrible secret.

When the princess heard that her beloved horse was to die, she went secretly to see the slaughterer. She promised him a piece of gold if he would nail the horse's head up in a dark gateway that she had to pass through every day with the geese, so she would be able to see it often. The man promised that he would.

The next morning, when the princess and the young boy passed through the gateway with the geese, she looked at her poor horse's head and said, "Alas, Falada! Hanging there."

The head answered her sadly. "Alas, Princess! How ill you fare. If your mother knew, her heart would break in two."

The two unlikely companions—the princess and the little boy who tended the geese—passed out of the town and herded the geese into the country until they reached a meadow. There, the princess sat down and unwound her hair from the tight braid she had put it in. It tumbled over her shoulders and gleamed like pure gold in the sunlight.

The little goose boy loved how bright and beautiful it was, and he longed to pull out some of the golden strands to keep for himself.

The princess saw his intentions, and she spoke under her breath. "Blow, blow gentle wind, I say, blow the goose boy's hat away. Make him chase it here and there, until I have braided up my hair."

As soon as she spoke, a gust of wind blew the boy's hat from his head, and he had to run about the field chasing after it. By the time he had caught it, the golden hair was wound back into a braid on top of the girl's head. The boy scowled at the princess and did not speak all the way home.

The next day, as they passed underneath the dark gateway with the geese, the princess once again spoke to the head of Falada. Again, he said, "Alas, Princess! How ill you fare. If your mother knew, her heart would break in two."

When they reached the meadow, the girl took down her golden hair again. As soon as she saw the boy reach out to pluck some of it, she said, "Blow, blow, gentle wind, I say. Blow the goose boy's hat away." Once more, the hat was snatched from his head, and he had to chase it about the field, while the girl combed her hair and tied it up again.

The boy was so angry that he went straight to the old king to complain about her. "I will not tend the geese with that girl any longer," he said crossly.

"Why not?" asked the king. "What on earth can such a dainty girl have done to upset you so much?"

The young boy told the king the whole story, about how the goose girl spoke every day to the horse's head mounted on the wall of the gateway, and about how she made him chase his hat through the fields. The king commanded him to carry on herding his flock of geese as normal. The very next day, the king hid himself in the shadow of the dark gateway to hear the girl talk to Falada. Then, he followed the two companions to the country and hid behind a tree in the meadow to watch what happened there. Sure enough, he saw the goose girl unwind her shining hair, heard her murmur softly, and watched as a gust of wind blew the goose boy's hat away across the field.

When he got back to the palace, the king called for the goose girl and asked her why she acted as she did. "Oh, Your Highness," she said, "I am sorry, but I cannot tell you why. I swore that I would never tell, and if I break my oath, I will surely be killed."

"Well," said the king, "if you can't tell me your troubles, then tell them to the iron stove over here."

The princess went over to the stove and poured out her heart, lamenting the cruelty of her maid. The old king had not left the room, however—he had merely hidden himself behind the door. As soon as he heard the truth, the king ordered that fine robes be brought to the princess.

When she was properly dressed, her beauty was dazzling. The king summoned his son to show him his true bride. The prince was overjoyed when he saw how lovely the princess was and ordered that a great feast be prepared.

The true princess was seated on one side of the prince, and the false bride was seated on the other. The false bride was so unused to seeing the princess that she didn't recognize her, and the meal was eaten with much merriment and happiness.

After the meal, the king asked the false princess what she thought should happen to cruel deceivers and liars. She thought about this for a while, and then said, "I think they should be banished and severely punished."

"Well, then," said the king, "you have just decided your own sentence. So be it." The punishment was carried out right away, and the prince and the princess were married at last.

The Dung Beetle

In the emperor's stables, there lived a great and magnificent horse, with bright eyes and a glossy chestnut mane.
The emperor had ridden him into battle many times and was very fond of him. As a reward for the horse's loyal service, the emperor ordered golden shoes to be made for him, commanding that they should be fitted immediately.

Now, the horse was not the only creature to live in the warm stables — there was also a dung beetle. When he saw the man coming to fit the horse with beautiful new shoes, the beetle grew very excited. He waited his turn impatiently, thinking that he, too, would be given golden shoes from the emperor.

When the man saw the beetle holding out his spindly leg for a fitting, he burst out laughing. "What on earth makes you think that you deserve shoes like these, Beetle?" he asked. "What good have you ever done anyone?"

The beetle was insulted by this. "What makes that creature any better than me? Why should he get special treatment?" he asked.

In a foul temper, he spread his wings and flew out of the stable.

After a while, he came to a lovely garden full of sweet-smelling flowers. There were many red and black ladybugs flying around and enjoying the sunshine. One of them smiled at the beetle as she passed him, saying, "How beautiful everything is. How wonderful it is to be alive!"

The dung beetle sneered at her. "So you think this is beautiful, do you?" he said, looking down his nose at her. "Where I come from everything is much finer and grander than all of this." And he flew away, leaving the poor ladybug feeling very dejected. The arrogant dung beetle landed on the grass of a well-kept lawn, and there he fell fast asleep.

Suddenly, the sky filled with black clouds, and heavy rain began to fall. The dung beetle was woken up with a shock, and did not have time to search for any shelter. The raindrops turned him this way and that until he thought he would have to swim for his life. After a time, he spotted something white on the grass nearby and scuttled toward it as best he could. It was a shirt that had fallen from a clothesline. The beetle crawled into a crease in the wet fabric and waited there until the rain had passed over. He stayed there, shivering, for a whole day and night, thinking of the warm, dry stables and feeling very sorry for himself.

As the rain began to ease up, the dung beetle poked his head out of the sleeve and saw that the shirt was also occupied by two very happy-looking frogs.

"Oh, how I do love this weather," said one. "It's so cooling and fresh."

"Yes, my friend," said the other. "Is there anything finer than a nice heavy rainfall?"

The beetle scuttled up to them. "You really don't know what you're talking about," he told them, in a loud voice. "I live in the stables of the emperor, where it is dry and warm, and there is nowhere better to live. You must be crazy if you think this horrible damp climate is better than that."

The two frogs did not like the dung beetle's tone, and they turned their backs on him. So, he flew off in search of somewhere he would feel more at home, thinking sadly about how ignorant everyone seemed to be.

He flew over a great many fields, houses, and gardens until he came to a ditch in which he found several other beetles. They were bathing in the rich, dark mud of the ditch, and they motioned for him to join them. He was glad to have the chance to rest his tired wings and happy to be among his own kind again.

Down in the ditch, there were, among others, three young lady beetles relaxing in the mud. The dung beetle thought that the eldest was really very beautiful and could not take his eyes off her. The girl's mother noticed him gazing at her daughter and whispered to him that she was not yet married. Well, in no time at all, the beetle had decided to make this young lady his wife, and there was much rejoicing in the ditch.

For the beetle, the first days of marriage were very happy and full of laughter. After the first week, however, he had begun to get bored of always being in the same company.

So, he secretly started to plan ways in which he could escape. He told his new wife that he was going to look for some food for them both to enjoy and flew off into the sky before she had a chance to complain. "Little does she know that I won't be coming back," he thought to himself cruelly. After a few days had passed, his wife realized that she had been abandoned, and she wept for many days.

The dung beetle was happy to continue his adventures. He flew here and there until he reached a greenhouse with an open window that was too tempting to resist. Inside, it was warm, and there were huge, green leaves and bright flowers of every color you can imagine. The beetle burrowed into some of the warm earth and made himself comfortable. "This is the kind of place I could feel at home in," he said to himself. "This is better even than the emperor's stables. The horse with his golden shoes could only dream of something as fine as this." He sighed with happiness.

Suddenly, a hand grabbed him from his comfortable earthy bed and squeezed him very tightly. It was the gardener's son, who had spotted the beetle and decided that he wanted to play. He wrapped the beetle up in a leaf and put him into his pocket. Every time the beetle tried to struggle or escape, he would get a knock on the head that made him dizzy and confused. The child took his new plaything to the edge of a lake, where he had fashioned a small boat from a wooden shoe, with a twig for a mast. The boy decided that the beetle should learn how to sail. So, he tipped the unfortunate beetle out of his pants pocket into the makeshift ship, tied him with string to the mast, and placed him on the lake to sail away.

The beetle was terrified. To him, the lake seemed like a never-ending sea. The little boat was pulled this way and that by the waves, and the beetle began to doubt he would ever see dry land again. He was very miserable. He thought about his experiences in the big wide world and decided that it was a cruel place. "First I was denied golden shoes and then I was soaked to the skin. Next I was saddled with the responsibility of a wife and finally, when I had just found a place for myself in the world, I am made a prisoner of a human child and sent to a watery end."

He continued to lament the sad state of his life as the little boat was rocked to and fro by the waves. All of a sudden, a much bigger boat came up to him. In it were three young girls. They saw the poor beetle's plight and felt sorry for him. One of the girls fished his little boat out of the lake and cut him loose with a pair of scissors, being careful not to injure his wings.

"Fly away, little beetle," she said kindly to him. "Be glad to have your freedom."

The dung beetle fluttered away and flew straight into the open window of a large wooden building. He landed in the silky mane of a huge horse. Looking down, he saw the sparkle of its golden shoes. He was home. Never had he been so glad to see the emperor's favorite horse, and he realized that his lot in life was not as bad as he had thought. He did not need golden shoes. He was safe and warm. The sun was shining, and it was a beautiful day. "I suppose the world is not as bad as I thought it was," he said to himself as he drifted off to sleep in the hay.

Stone Soup

Once upon a time, in a far-off land, three soldiers were walking wearily down a lonely and dusty road. They were on their journey home from a long and fierce battle and had been traveling without rest for many days. All three of them were hot, tired, and hungry.

"How I wish we could find a hot meal to eat tonight," lamented the first soldier.

"Yes," agreed the second man. "I would love to have a soft, warm bed to sleep in tonight."

"Ah, my friends," said the third. "We have not seen another man for miles — I fear your wishes are impossible."

They trudged onward in silence, each thinking of the things he lacked and the comfort he craved. Suddenly, one of the soldiers noticed lights up ahead, and they realized that they were approaching a village.

"Maybe there will be someone here who will be able to give us some dinner and a place to sleep," they thought, and quickened their pace toward the village.

The people of the village were not rich men and women, but they had enough to get by. There was always food on the table, so no one went hungry. They were a happy community, but they were very distrustful of strangers. When the news came that there were three soldiers approaching their village, they called a conference. "Soldiers are always hungry," they said. "If we give them food, then we will not be able to eat our fill and we might be hungry tonight." This was a worrying thought, and so, they decided to hide the food that they had in and around their houses.

They hurried to hide loaves of bread under beds. Vegetables were stuffed behind furniture, and the villagers even lowered buckets of fresh milk down the well in the village square. Once everything edible was safely hidden away out of sight, they waited for the soldiers to arrive.

The hungry soldiers came to the first house and knocked at the door. When the man of the house came to the door, all three of them smiled politely. "Good evening, sir," they said. "We are very sorry to disturb you, but we are so hungry and tired. Do you perhaps have some food that you could spare to feed three hungry soldiers?"

"I'm sorry," lied the man. "In my house, we haven't even got enough to feed ourselves and our children. The harvest was very poor this year."

The soldiers thanked him and moved on sadly to the next house. "Excuse me, madam," they said to the woman who answered the door. "We are so tired and hungry. Is there a corner that we could sleep in for the night?"

"I'm afraid not," the old woman lied. "All of the beds in this house are full. We have no space for soldiers."

Every house that the poor soldiers tried gave them the same answer. No one had anything to spare — no food, no beds, and no space. All of the villagers swore that they did not have enough food even to feed their own families. The soldiers understood their reasons, but by now they were so hungry that they decided to try to persuade the people of the village one last time.

Together they gathered in the village square and called out as loudly as they could, "Good citizens of this village, we thank you for listening to our plight. We are very hungry and far from home. We came to ask for food, but it seems that you have none to spare, so we are left with no other choice." They looked at one another with a twinkle in their eyes. "We will have to make stone soup to eat."

The villagers heard this, but could not believe their ears. A murmur went around the village that here were some men who could make soup from stones, and a crowd gathered in the village square. The soldiers asked the villagers for a large metal pot. They filled it with water and then lit a fire underneath it to heat it up. Then, as all of the villagers watched, one of the soldiers produced three large, smooth stones and dropped them into the pot.

The first soldier began stirring the soup in the pot, smelling the steam every few seconds and making approving noises. "Now, stones on their own make quite a good soup, but if you want a really good soup, we'll need salt and pepper to add extra flavor."

When they heard this, some of the children ran to fetch salt and pepper from their kitchen to help the soldiers with their soup.

Then the second soldier piped up, "Of course, if we had a few carrots, we could make this even better."

Right away, a woman's voice could be heard. "Do you know, I think I may have a few carrots somewhere," she said, and ran to her pantry to get them.

"Some of the best stone soups use cabbage, too," said the third hungry soldier. "But I know how poor your harvest was, so we won't ask for what we know we can't have."

There was silence for a while, and then a man said, "If I look hard enough, I might be able to find some cabbage."

The soldiers looked at one another. "What would make this a really superior stone soup would be if we could find some beef and a few potatoes," one said, licking his lips.

Sure enough, several men and women scurried off to their homes to bring out their food from its hiding place. It was true that they didn't have much, but they thought it was worth it to see these men create soup from only a few stones.

"Our soup is almost finished," said the first soldier. "It smells delicious. If only we had some barley and some milk, we could make this the best stone soup that has ever been tasted."

The soldiers were not at all surprised to find pails of milk and handfuls of barley being thrust into their hands by the villagers to use in their "magic" soup. They added all of the ingredients and let the soup bubble and thicken in the pot. It really did smell delicious, and the hungry soldiers could hardly wait to eat it. Finally, it was ready. "Our soup is finished, and there's enough for everyone," they told the villagers.

With much hustle and bustle, great wooden tables were set up in the middle of the village. As the soldiers ladled out steaming bowlfuls of the soup, some of the villagers fetched loaves of bread and bottles of cider to enjoy with it. Soon, everyone was sitting on long, low benches and digging into the soup with much merriment. The food was the most delicious that the villagers had ever tasted.

When the banquet was finished, the soldiers yawned and prepared to curl up in the village square to sleep. "This will never do," said the people of the village. "You brilliant and clever chefs must have the best beds we have to offer." As if by magic, each of the soldiers was given a soft, warm bed in the house of one of the village families. Never had they had such a good night's sleep.

The Tortoise and the Hare
(Adapted from the fable by Aesop)

There was once a hare who loved nothing more than to run through the fields. He spent all day running from one place to the next, and he was sure that he was by far the fastest of all the animals. "I could beat anyone in a race," he would boast. "There is no one on earth who is quite as fast as me."

His neighbor, the tortoise, soon grew tired of the hare's arrogance. He decided to teach the boastful animal a lesson. "I challenge you to a race tomorrow. We'll see if you're as fast as you say you are."

The hare thought this was the funniest thing he had ever heard. He laughed until tears ran down his face. "All right, old man," he said. "I accept your challenge. This will be the easiest race I have ever won."

They agreed upon a course and marked the start and finish lines. When the time came to start the race, the hare could not help laughing once again at the thought of being beaten by the plodding old tortoise. Sure enough, he shot off into the distance, leaving the tortoise far behind him.

"This is too easy," the confident hare thought. Seeing a soft patch of long grass beside the track, he decided to have a quick nap. "I should at least give the poor tortoise a sporting chance," he thought. "I'll just rest for a few minutes." He lay down in the long grass, closed his eyes, and fell into a deep sleep.

All this time, the tortoise kept trudging toward the finish line. When he reached the sleeping hare, he smiled and tiptoed past him.

After a long while, the hare opened his eyes with a start. He had no idea how long he had been asleep. He scrambled to his feet and sprinted off toward the finish line as fast as he could. To his horror, he saw the tortoise was already there, leaning against a fence and waving at him. He had been beaten! As he crossed the finish line, he heard the tortoise call out to him, "You see, it takes more than speed to win some races."

ALSO AVAILABLE:

The Fairy Tale Book

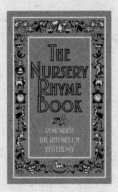

The Nursery Rhyme Book

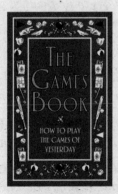

The Games Book

Also available in this bestselling series: